"That's a good question. Well, why don't we see? Hold my hand tightly, Avery, stay close to me."

"The squirrels like stories at bedtime, it seems. I'll bet it's a tale that will give them sweet dreams."

Avery's Countdown to Bedtime

10 Put away your toys

9 Take a bath

8 Brush your teeth

7 Use the bathroom

6 Wash your hands

Written by J.D. Green
Illustrated by Joanne Partis
Designed by Ryan Dunn

Copyright © Bidu Bidu Books Ltd. 2024

Put Me In The Story is a
registered trademark of Sourcebooks.
All rights reserved.

Published by Put Me In The Story,
a publication of Sourcebooks.
P.O. Box 4410, Naperville, Illinois 60567-4410
(630) 536-1104
putmeinthestory.com

Date of Production: July 2023
Run Number: 5032755
Printed and bound in China (GD)
10 9 8 7 6 5 4 3 2 1